RUMI

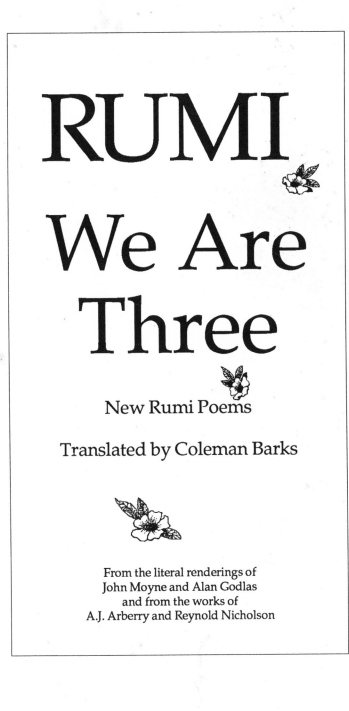

We Are Three

New Rumi Poems

Translated by Coleman Barks

From the literal renderings of
John Moyne and Alan Godlas
and from the works of
A.J. Arberry and Reynold Nicholson

MAYPOP BOOKS

RUMI: We Are Three

$7.50 / copy, plus $1.00 postage and handling,
25¢ each additional book.
Order from
Coleman Barks
196 Westview Drive
Athens, GA 30606
tel. 404-543-2148
Second printing, with additional poems.

ISBN: 0-9618916-0-2

This collection of Rumi
is meant as a gift
to friends in the Bay Area.

I felt such generosity
and love and genuine enthusiasm
for Rumi
during my recent (September 1986)
series of readings there.

Thank you.

Introductory Notes

Rumi's Life (1207-1273)

Jalaluddin Rumi was born in Balkh (Afghanistan), of a long lineage of scholars, jurists and theologians. His family fled the Mongol invasions and settled in Konya (Turkey), where he eventually succeeded his father as head of the *medrese*, the dervish learning community. This fairly conventional career, however, changed completely when, at thirty-seven, he met Shams of Tabriz. "What I thought of before as God, I met today in a person." With Shams he discovered the inner Friend, the soul, the Beloved, a constant reminder of God's presence. However one might try to name that mystery, out of its love-joy-longing came the poetry, the turning (Rumi was the original "whirling dervish"), and the surrender that continues to ignite, and unite, lives.

Hallaj (p.1)

What Hallaj said was Ana'l-Haqq. ("I am the Truth," or "I am the Reality," or "I am God.") This claim brought about his execution for heresy in Baghdad in 922 A.D.

sohbet (p. 4)

This word has no English equivalent. It means something like "mystical conversation on mystical subjects." It refers to the communion that Rumi and Shams enjoyed.

hornet-nafs (p.42)

Nafs is an Arabic word with many levels of meaning.
Perhaps the simplest is "desires, impulsive needs and
wantings." You might say adolescent boys are driven by
nafs. But in the Sufi traditions nafs take more subtle
forms. There are nafs of gentleness, nafs of adoration,
and nafs of spiritual surrender. Each stage of growth
has its nafs which make one satisfied with his present
state and inhibit further growth. Recognition of, and
conflict with, those nafs (as with the hornets in the
poem), lead to an opening, a new breathing, the next
step. Nafs can also mean "ego," or "self," as well as
"breath." At even more subtle levels, it is connected
with Nur, the Divine Light.

Zikr (p. 42)

Zikr (or dhikr) means remembrance. In a practical sense
it refers to the internal or external repetition of the
phrase,

La 'illaha il' Allahu (There is nothing other thanYou,
O God. You alone are God).

It is an inspiration for the orthodox and unorthodox
alike, and a conundrum as well. On one level it is an
affirmation of monotheism, like the Jewish creed:
"Hear oh Israel, the Lord thy God is One God." Others
take it to mean that in everything is God, God is the
only Reality.

The Zikr is said to have at least three parts. The first

part, *La illaha,* is the denial, the denial of everything, abandonment, the depths. The second part, *il'Allah,* is the actual intrusion, explosion into the individual, of the Divine Presence. *Hu,* the third part, is the Out-Breathing of That.

One Sufi teacher, Bawa Muhaiyaddeen, advised his students to repeat and reflect upon the *zikr* with every breath. A student asked the teacher, "But how is that possible, I mean, how could anyone do that?" The teacher smiled and said, "It is like driving a car. At first you think it is difficult, but you get used to it. It becomes natural. After awhile, you can even drive and talk at the same time."

The sura called *Daybreak* (p. 59)

Say: I seek refuge
With the Lord of the Dawn,

From the mischief
Of created things;

From the mischief
Of those who practise
Secret Arts:

And from the mischief
Of the envious one
As he practises envy.

(translation by A. Yusef Ali)

These translations are collaborations with several other sources: A.J. Arberry, (pp. 1,3, 7-9, 14,16, 20-21, 24-25), Reynold Nicholson (pp. 4-6, 10-13, 17-19, 26-55, 58-59, 67-86), Alan Godlas (pp.2, 22-23), and John Moyne (pp. 15, 56-57, 60-66).

John Moyne and I have also collaborated on two other books of Rumi's poetry:
Open Secret — $7.00 (Quatrains, odes, and sections from the Mathnawi)
Unseen Rain — $8.00 (Quatrains).

These are available from: Threshold Books
RD #3
Box 1350
Putney, VT 05346

A larger collection of other Rumi poems that I am working on with Robert Bly is in the final stages of preparation. It will come out from Harper and Row and a selection of Rumi odes, not included in any of these books, will be published by Copper Beech Press.

Coleman Barks

May 2, 1987

Hallaj said what he said and went to the Origin
through the hole in the scaffold.

I cut a cap's worth of cloth from his robe,
and it swamped over me from head to foot.

Years ago, I broke a bunch of roses
from the top of his wall. A thorn from that
is still in my palm, working deeper.

From Hallaj, I learned to hunt lions,
but I became something hungrier than a lion.

I was a frisky colt. He broke me
with a quiet hand on the side of my head.

A person comes to him naked. It's cold.
There's a fur coat floating in the river.

"Jump in and get it," he says.
You dive in. You reach for the coat.
It reaches for you.

It's a live bear that has fallen in upstream,
drifting with the current.

"How long does it take!" Hallaj yells from the bank.
"Don't wait," you answer. "This coat has decided
to wear me home!"

A little part of a story, a hint.
Do you need long sermons on Hallaj!

(#1288)

1

I was a tiny bug. Now a mountain.
I was left behind. Now honored at the head.

You healed my wounded hunger and anger,
and made me a poet who sings about joy.

(#1966)

I never get enough of laughing with you,
that wild humor.

Thirsty and dry, I complain, but everything is made of
                    water!
Lonely, yet my head leans against your shirt!
My wounded hands, your hands.

Do something drastic.

You say, "Come and sit in the innermost room,
where you'll be safe from the love-thief."

I reply, "But I've tried to be the ringknocker
on your door, so you won't have to
always be letting me in and out."

You say, "No. You stand on the threshold waiting,
and you're here in the inner chamber too.
You're at home in both places."

I love the quietness of such an answer.
Come to this table of quietness.

(#2244)

A

mouse and a frog meet every morning
on the riverbank.
They sit in a nook of the ground and talk.

Each morning, the second they see each other,
they open easily, telling stories and dreams and secrets,
empty of any fear or suspicious holding-back.

To watch and listen to these two
is to understand how, as it's written,
sometimes when two beings come together,
Christ becomes visible.

The mouse starts laughing out a story he hasn't thought of
in five years, and the telling might take five years!
There's no blocking the speechflow-river-running-
all-carrying momentum
that true intimacy is.

Bitterness doesn't have a chance
with those two.

The God-Messenger, Khidr, touches a roasted fish.
It leaps off the grill
back into the water.

Friend sits by Friend, and the tablets appear.
They read the mysteries
off each other's foreheads.

But one day the mouse complains, "There are times
when I want *sohbet*, and you're out in the water,
jumping around where you can't hear me.

4

We meet at this appointed time,
but the text says, *Lovers pray constantly.*

Once a day, once a week, five times an hour,
is not enough. Fish like we are
need the ocean around us!"

Do camel-bells say, *Let's meet back here*
    Thursday night?
Ridiculous. They jingle
together continuously,
talking while the camel walks.

Do you pay regular visits to *yourself?*
Don't argue or answer rationally.

Let us die,
                   and dying, reply.

(*Mathnawi*, VI, 2632, 2665-2669, 2681-2684)

5

I am part of the load
not rightly balanced.
I drop off in the grass,
like the old Cave-sleepers, to browse
wherever I fall.

For hundreds of thousands of years I have been dust-grains
floating and flying in the will of the air,
often forgetting ever being
in that state, but in sleep
I migrate back. I spring loose
from the four-branched, time-and-space cross,
this waiting room.

I walk into a huge pasture.
I nurse the milk of millennia.

Everyone does this in different ways.
Knowing that conscious decisions
and personal memory
are much too small a place to live,
every human being streams at night
into the loving nowhere, or during the day,
in some absorbing work.

(*Mathnawi*, VI, 216-227)

I magine the time the particle you are
returns where it came from!

The family darling comes home. Wine, without being contained
in cups, is handed around.

A red glint appears in a granite outcrop,
and suddenly the whole cliff turns to ruby.

At dawn I walked along with a monk on his way to the
                    monastery.
"We do the same work," I told him. "We suffer the same."

He gave me a bowl.
And I saw:

The soul has *this* shape.

                    Shams,
and actual sunlight,

                    help me now,

being in the middle of being partly in my self,
and partly outside.

(#2805)

This mirror inside me shows...
I can't say what, but I can't not know!

I run from body. I run from spirit.
I do not belong anywhere.

I'm not alive!
You smell the decay?

You talk about my craziness.
Listen rather to the honed-blade sanity I say.

This gourd-head on top of a dervish robe,
do I look like someone you know?

This dipper gourd full of liquid,
upsidedown and not spilling a drop!

Or if it spills, it drops into God
and rounds into pearls.

I form a cloud over that ocean
and gather spillings.

When Shams is here,
I rain.

After a day or two, lilies sprout,
the shape of my tongue.

(#1486)

Only union with you gives joy.
The rest is tearing down one building
to put up another.
                    But don't break
with forms!

Boats cannot move without water.
We are misquoted texts
made right when you say us.

We are sheep in a tightening wolf-circle:
You come like a shepherd and ask,
                    "So how are you?"
I start crying.

This means something to anyone in a body,
but what *means* something to you?

You can't be spoken, though you listen
to all sound. You can't be written,
but you read everything.

You don't sleep, yet you're the source of dream-vision.

Your ship glides over nothing,
deep silence, praise for the ONE,
who told Moses on Sinai,

                    You Shall Not See Me

(#2756)

Little by little, wean yourself.

This is the gist of what I have to say.

From an embryo, whose nourishment comes in the blood,
move to an infant drinking milk,
to a child on solid food,
to a searcher after wisdom,
to a hunter of more invisible game.

Think how it is to have a conversation with an embryo.
You might say, "The world outside is vast and intricate.
There are wheatfields and mountain passes, and orchards in bloc

At night there are millions of galaxies, and in sunlight
the beauty of friends dancing at a wedding."

You ask the embryo why he, or she, stays cooped up
in the dark with eyes closed.

                              Listen to the answer.

There is no "other world."
I only know what I've experienced.
You must be hallucinating.

(*Mathnawi*, III, 49-62)

A

man gives one coin to be spent among four people.

The Persian says, "I want *angur*."
The Arab says, "*Inab*, you rascal."
The Turk says, "*Uzum!*"
The Greek says, "Shut up all of you.
We'll have *istafil*."

They begin pushing each other about,
then hitting each other with their fists, no stopping it.

If a many-languaged master had been there,
He could have made peace and told them:
I can give each of you what you want
with this one coin. Trust me, keep quiet,
and you four enemies will agree.

I know a silent, inner meaning
that makes of your four words one wine.

(*Mathnawi*, II, 3681-3692)

A chickpea leaps almost over the rim of the pot
where it's being boiled.

"Why are you doing this to me?"

The cook knocks it down with the ladle.

"Don't you try to jump out.
You think I'm torturing you,
I'm giving you flavor,
so you can mix with spices and rice
and be the lovely vitality of a human being.

Remember when you drank rain in the garden.
That was for this."

Grace first. Sexual pleasure,
then a boiling new life begins,
and the Friend has something good to eat.

(*Mathnawi*, III, 4160-4168)

These spiritual windowshoppers,
who idly ask, *How much is that? Oh, I'm just looking.*
They handle a hundred items and put them down,
shadows with no capital.

What is spent is love and two eyes wet with weeping.
But these walk into a shop,
and their whole lives pass suddenly in that moment,
in that shop.

Where did you go? "Nowhere."
What did you have to eat? "Nothing much."

Even if you don't know what you want,
buy *something*, to be part of the exchanging flow.

Start a huge, foolish, project,
like Noah.

It makes absolutely no difference
what people think of you.

(*Mathnawi*, VI, 831-845)

I used to want buyers for my words.
Now I wish someone would buy me away from words.

I've made a lot of charmingly profound images,
scenes with Abraham, and Abraham's father, Azar,
who was also famous for icons.

I'm so tired of what I've been doing.

Then one image without form came,
and I quit.

Look for someone else to tend the shop.
I'm out of the image-making business.

Finally I know the freedom
of madness.

A random image arrives. I scream,
"Get out!" It disintegrates.

Only love.
Only the holder the flag fits into,
and wind. No flag.

(#2449)

When you are with everyone but me,
         you're with no one.
When you are with no one but me, you're with everyone.

Instead of being so bound up *with* everyone, *be* everyone.
When you become that many, you're nothing. Empty.

(#1793)

My love wanders the rooms, melodious,
flute-notes, plucked wires,
full of a wine the Magi drank
on the way to Bethlehem.

We are three. The moon comes
from its quiet corner, puts a pitcher of water
down in the center. The circle
of surface flames.

One of us kneels to kiss the threshold.

One drinks, with wine-flames playing over his face.

One watches the gathering,

and says to any cold onlookers,

This dance is the joy of existence.

(#2395)

Some people work and become wealthy.
Others do the same and remain poor.

Marriage fills one with energy.
Another it drains.

Don't trust ways. They change.
A means flails about like a donkey's tail.

Always add the gratitude clause
to any sentence, *if God wills,*
then go.

You may be leading a donkey, no,
a goat, no, who can tell?

We sit in a dark pit and think we're home.
We pass around delicacies.
Poisoned bait.

You think this is preachy doubletalk?

Those who do not breathe the *God willing* phrase
live in a collective blindness.

Rubbing their eyes, they ask the dark,
"Who's there?"

(*Mathnawi,* VI, 3685-3698)

17

A peaceful face twists with the poisonous nail
of thinking. A golden spade
sinks into a pile of shit.

Suppose you loosen an intellectual knot.
The sack is empty. You've grown old
trying to untie such difficulties.
So loosen a few more, why knot!

There is a big one fastened at your throat,
the problem of whether you're in harmony
with that which has no definition.
Try solving that.

You examine substance and accidents.
You waste your life making subject and verb agree.
You edit hearsay.

You study artifacts and think you know the Maker,
so proud of having thought that syllogism.

A thinker collects and links up proofs.
A mystic does the opposite.
He lays his head on a person's chest
and sinks into the answer.

Thinking gives off smoke
to prove the existence of fire.
The mystic sits within the burning.

Imagination loves to discover shapes
in rising smoke, but it's a great mistake
to leave the fire for that filmy sight.

(*Mathnawi*, V, 557-573)

Paradoxes: Best wakefulness in sleep, wealth
in having nothing, a pearl necklace
fastened around an iron collar.
Fire contained in boiling water.

Revenues growing from funds flowing *out*.
Giving is gainful employment.
It brings in money.

Taking time for ritual prayer and meditation
saves time. Sweet fruits
hide in leaves.

Dung becomes food
for the ground, and generative
power in trees.

Non-existence contains existence.
Love encloses beauty.
Dark brown flint and gray steel
have candlelight in them.

Inside fear, safety.
In the black pupil of the eye,
many brilliancies.

Inside the body-cow,
a handsome prince.

(*Mathnawi*, VI, 3567-3581)

What I want is to see your face
in a tree, in the sun coming out,
in the air.

What I want is
to hear the falcon-drum, and light again
on your forearm.

You say, "Tell him I'm not here." The sound
of that brusque dismissal
becomes what I want.

To see in every palm your elegant silver coin-shavings,
to turn with the wheel of the rain,
to fall with the falling bread

of every experience,
to swim like a huge fish
in ocean water,

to be Jacob recognizing Joseph.
To be a desert mountain
instead of a city.

I'm tired of cowards.
I want to live with lions.
With Moses.

Not whining, teary people. I want
the ranting of drunkards.
I want to sing like birds sing,

not worrying who hears,
            or what they think.
                        Last night,

a great teacher went from door to door
            with a lamp. "He who is not to be found
                        is the one I'm looking for."

Beyond wanting, beyond place, inside form,
            That One. A flute says, *I have no hope*
                        for finding that.

But Love plays
            and is the music played.
                        Let that musician

finish this poem. Shams,
            I am a waterbird
                        flying into the sun.

(#441)

No longer a stranger, you
listen all day to these crazy love-words.
Like a bee you fill hundreds of homes with honey,
though yours is a long flight from here.

(#1618)

A drunk comes in off the road with a flask.
The cup going round and round, hand to hand,
suddenly slips, shatters.
Cups don't last long among drunks.

(#415)

Some huge work goes on growing,
or not growing.
How could one person's words matter?

Where you walk, heads pop from the ground.
What is one seed-head compared to you?

On my death-day I'll know the answer.

I have cleared this house,
so your furniture, when it comes,
can fill every room.

I slide like an empty boat pulled over the water.

(#622)

24

We can't help being thirsty,
moving toward the voice
of water.

Milk-drinkers draw close
to the mother. Muslims, Christians, Jews,
Buddhists, Hindus, shamans,
everyone hears the intelligent sound
and moves, with thirst, to meet it.

Clean your ears. Don't listen
for something you've heard before.

Invisible camel bells,
slight footfalls in sand.

Almost in sight! The first word they call out
will be the last word of our last poem.

(#837)

I have been tricked by flying too close
to what I thought I loved.

Now the candleflame is out, the wine spilled,
and the lovers have withdrawn
somewhere beyond my squinting.

The amount I thought I'd won, I've lost.
My prayer becomes bitter and all about blindness.

How wonderful it was to be for a while
with those who surrender.

Others only turn their faces one way,
then another, like pigeons in flight.

I have known pigeons who fly in a nowhere,
and birds that eat grainlessness,

and tailors who sew beautiful clothes
by tearing them to pieces.

(*Mathnawi*, V, 346-353)

Your grief for what you've lost lifts a mirror
up to where you're bravely working.

Expecting the worst, you look and instead,
here's the joyful face you've been wanting to see.

Your hand opens and closes and opens and closes.
If it were always a fist or always stretched open,
you would be paralyzed.

Your deepest presence is in every small contracting and expanding,
the two as beautifully balanced and coordinated
as birdwings.

(*Mathnawi*, III, 3769-3766)

A friend remarks to the Prophet, "Why is it
I get screwed in business deals?
It's like a spell. I become distracted
by business talk and make wrong decisions."

Muhammad replies, "Stipulate with every transaction
that you need three days to make sure."

Deliberation is one of the qualities of God.
Throw a dog a bit of something.
He sniffs to see if he wants it.

Be that careful.
Sniff with your wisdom-nose.
Get clear. Then decide.

The universe came into being gradually
over six days. God could have just commanded,
Be!

Little by little a person reaches forty and fifty and sixty,
and feels more complete. God could have thrown
                full-blown prophets
flying through the cosmos in an instant.

Jesus said one word, and a dead man sat up,
but Creation usually unfolds,
like calm breakers.

Constant, slow movement teaches us to keep working
like a small creek that stays clear,
that doesn't stagnate, but finds a way
through numerous details, deliberately.

Deliberation is born of joy,
like a bird from an egg.

                              Birds don't resemble eggs!
Think how different the hatching out is.

A white-leathery snake egg, a sparrow's egg;
a quince seed, an apple seed: Very different things
look similar at one stage.

These leaves, our bodily personalities, seem identical,
but the globe of soul-fruit
we make,
each is elaborately
unique.

(Mathnawi, III, 3494-3516)

Someone said, "there is no dervish, or if there is a dervish,
that dervish is not there."

Look at a candleflame in bright noon sunlight.
If you put cotton next to it, the cotton will burn,
but its light has become completely mixed
with the sun.

That candlelight you can't find   is what's left of a dervish.

If you sprinkle one ounce of vinegar over
two hundred tons of sugar,
no one will ever taste the vinegar.

A deer faints in the paws of a lion. The deer becomes
another glazed expression on the face of the lion.

These are rough metaphors for what happens to the lover.

There's no one more openly irreverent than a lover. He, or she,
jumps up on the scale opposite eternity
and claims to balance it.

And no one more secretly reverent.

A grammar lesson: "The lover died."
"Lover" is subject and agent, but that can't be!
The "lover" is defunct.

Only grammatically is the dervish-lover a doer.

In reality, with he or she so overcome,
        so dissolved into love,
                all qualities of doing-ness
                        disappear.

(*Mathnawi*, III, 3669-3685)

There once was a sneering wife
who ate all her husband brought home
and lied about it.

One day it was some lamb for a guest
who was to come. He had worked two hundred days
in order to buy that meat.

When he was away, his wife cooked a kabob
and ate it all, with wine.

The husband returns with the guest.
"The cat has eaten the meat," she says.
"Buy more, if you have any money left!"

He asks a servant to bring the scales,
and the cat. The cat weighs three pounds.
"The meat was three pounds, one ounce.
If this is the cat, where is the meat?
If this is the meat, where is the cat?
Start looking for one or the other!"

If you have a body, where is the spirit?
If you're spirit, what is the body?

This is not our problem to worry about.
Both are both. Corn is corn-grain and cornstalk.
The Divine Butcher cuts us a piece from the thigh,
and a piece from the neck.

Invisible, visible, the world
does not work without both.

If you throw dust at someone's head, nothing will
          happen.
If you throw water, nothing.
But combine them into a lump. That marriage
of water and dirt cracks open the head,
and afterwards there are other marriages.

(*Mathnawi*, V, 3409-3429)

H

ow could anyone resent sunlight?
Keep walking in this spaciousness
where the sun's flame is a white hawk.

But there *is* something flying higher.
Notice how you say *not* more.
Not this, *not* that. I do *not* know.

Negation points to affirmation.
Say rather what completely is.

(*Mathnawi*, VI, 634-641)

The core of masculinity does not derive from being
male,
nor friendliness from those who console.

Your old grandmother says,
"Maybe you shouldn't go to school.
You look a little pale."

Run when you hear that.
A father's stern slaps are better.

Your bodily soul wants comforting.
The severe father wants spiritual clarity.
He scolds, but eventually
leads you into the open.

Pray for a tough instructor
to hear and act and stay within you.

We have been busy accumulating solace.
Make us afraid of how we were.

(*Mathnawi*, VI, 1430-1445)

I need a mouth as wide as the sky
to say the nature of a True Person, language
as large as longing.

The fragile vial inside me often breaks.
No wonder I go mad and disappear for three days
every month with the moon.

For anyone in love with you,
it's always these invisible days.

I've lost the thread of the story I was telling.
My elephant roams his dream of Hindustan again.
Narrative, poetics, destroyed, my body,
a dissolving, a return.

Friend, I've shrunk to a hair trying to say your story.
Would you tell mine?
I've made up so many love stories.
Now I feel fictional.
Tell me!
The truth is, you are speaking, not me.
I am Sinai, and you are Moses walking there.
This poetry is an echo of what you say.
A piece of land can't speak, or know anything!
Or if it can, only within limits.

The body is a device to calculate
the astronomy of the spirit.
Look through that astrolabe
and become oceanic.

Why this distracted talk?
It's not my fault I rave.
You did this.
Do you approve of my love-madness?

Say yes.
What language will you say it in, Arabic or Persian,
or what? Once again, I must be tied up.
Bring the curly ropes of your hair.

                    Now I remember the story.
A True Man stares at his old shoes
and sheepskin jacket. Everyday he goes up
to his attic to look at his work-shoes and worn-out coat.
This is his wisdom, to remember the original clay
and not get drunk with ego and arrogance.

To visit those shoes and jacket
is praise.

The Absolute works with nothing.
The workshop, the materials,
are what does not exist.

Try and be a sheet of paper with nothing on it.
Be a spot of ground where nothing is growing,
where something might be planted,
a seed, possibly, from the Absolute.

(*Mathnawi*, V, 1884-1920, 1959-1964)

One day a Sufi sees an empty food-sack hanging on a nail.
He begins to turn and tear his shirt, saying,
Food for what needs no food!
A cure for hunger!

His burning grows and others join him,
shouting and moaning in the love-fire.

An idle passerby-by comments, "It's only an empty sack."

The Sufi says, *Leave. You want what we do not want.*
You are not a lover.

A lover's food is the love of bread,
not the bread. No one who really loves,
loves existence.

Lovers have nothing to do with existence.
They collect the interest without the capital.

No wings, yet they fly all over the world. No hands,
but they carry the polo ball from the field.

That dervish got a sniff of reality.
Now he weaves baskets of pure vision.

Lovers pitch tents on a field of Nowhere.
They are all one color like that field.

A nursing baby does not know the taste of roasted meat.
To a spirit the foodless scent is food.

To an Egyptian, the Nile looks bloody.
To an Israelite, clear.
What is a highway to one is disaster to the other.

(*Mathnawi*, III, 3014-3030)

M

y mention of Moses may block the message,
if you think I refer to something in the past.

The light of Moses is *here* and *now*, inside you.
Pharoah as well. The ceramic lamp and wick change,
but the light's the same. If you keep focusing
on the translucent chimney that surrounds the flame,
you will see only the Many, the colors
and their variations. Focus on a light within
the flame. You are that.

Where you perceive from should not change what you
                    perceive,
unless you're in a dark room.

Some Hindus brought an elephant to exhibit.
They kept it in an unlit house. Many people came and went
through the darkness. They couldn't see anything,
so they felt with their hands. One person's palm
touched the trunk. "It's like the downspout on a roof."
One felt an ear. "More like a fan."
The leg. "I find it round and solid like the column on a temple."
One touches the back. "An enormous throne."

One says *straight*, another *crooked*.
If each had a candle, differences would disappear.

Sense-knowledge is the way the palm knows the elephant
in the total pitchdark. A palm can't know the whole animal
at once. The Ocean has an eye. The foam-bubbles of phenomena
see differently. We bump against each other,
asleep in the bottom of our bodies' boats.

We should try to wake up and look with the clear Eye
of the water we float upon.

(*Mathnawi*, III, 1251-1274)

A naked man jumps in the river, hornets swarming
above him. The water is the *zikr*, remembering,
There is no Reality but God. There is only God.

The hornets are his sexual remembering, this woman,
that woman. Or if a woman, this man, that.
The head comes up. They sting.

Breathe water. Become river head to foot.
Hornets leave you alone then. Even if you're far from the river,
they pay no attention. No one looks for stars when the sun's out
A person blended into God does not disappear. He, or she,
is just completely soaked in God's qualities.
Do you need a quote from the Qur'an?

   All shall be brought into our Presence.

Join those travelers. The lamps we burn go out,
some quickly. Some last till daybreak.
Some are dim, some intense, all fed with fuel.

If a light goes out in one house, that doesn't affect
the next house. This is the story of the animal soul,
not the divine soul. The sun shines on every house.
When it goes down, all houses get dark.

Light is the image of your teacher. Your enemies
love the dark. A spider weaves a web over a light,
out of himself, or herself, makes a veil.

42

Don't try to control a wild horse by grabbing its leg.
Take hold the neck. Use a bridle. Be sensible.
Then ride! There is a need for self-denial.

Don't be contemptuous of old obediences. They help.

(*Mathnawi*, IV, 435-466)

Whir you do things from your soul,
you feel a river moving in you, a joy.

When actions come from another section,
the feeling disappears.

Don't let others lead you. They may be blind,
or worse, vultures. Reach for the rope
of God. And what is that?

Putting aside self-will.

Because of willfulness people sit in jail.
From willfulness, the trapped birds' wings are tied.
From willfulness, the fish sizzles in the skillet.

The anger of police is willfulness. You've seen
a magistrate inflict visible punishment.
Now see the invisible.

If you could leave selfishness, you would see
how your soul has been tortured.

We are born and live inside black water in a well.
How could we know what an open field of sunlight is?

Don't insist on going where you think you want to go.
Ask the way to the Spring.

Your living pieces will form a harmony.

There is a moving palace that floats through the air,
with balconies and clear water running in every part of it,
infinity everywhere, yet contained under a single tent.

(*Mathnawi*, VI, 3487-3510)

Someone who doesn't know the Tigris River exists
brings the Caliph who lives near the river
a jar of fresh water. The Caliph accepts, thanks him,
and gives in return a jar filled with gold coins.

"Since this man has come through the desert,
he should return by water." Taken out by another door,
the man steps into a waiting boat
and sees the wide freshwater of the Tigris.
He bows his head, "What wonderful kindness
that he took my gift."

Every object and being in the universe is
a jar overfilled with wisdom and beauty,
a drop of the Tigris that cannot be contained
by any skin. Every jarful spills and makes the earth
more shining, as though covered in satin.
If the man had seen even a tributary
of the great river, he wouldn't have brought
the innocence of his gift.

Those that stay and live by the Tigris
grow so ecstatic that they throw rocks at the jugs,
and the jugs become perfect!
                              They shatter.
The pieces dance, and water....
                              Do you see?
Neither jar, nor water, nor stone,
                              nothing.

You knock at the door of Reality.
You shake your thought-wings, loosen
your shoulders,
                    and open.

(*Mathnawi*, I, 2850-2870)

Here are the miracle-signs you want: That
you cry through the night and get up at dawn, asking,
that in the absence of what you ask for your day gets dark,
your neck thin as a spindle, that what you give away
is all you own, that you sacrifice belongings,
sleep, health, your head, that you often
sit down in a fire like aloes-wood, and often go out
to meet a blade like a battered helmet.

When acts of helplessness become habitual,
those are the *signs*.

But you run back and forth listening for unusual events,
peering into the faces of travelers.
"Why are you looking at me like a madman?"
I have lost a Friend. Please forgive me.

Searching like that does not fail.
There will come a rider who holds you close.
You faint and gibber. The uninitiated say, "He's faking."
How could they know?
Water washes over a beached fish, the water
of those signs I just mentioned.

Excuse my wandering.
How can one be orderly with this?
It's like counting leaves in a garden,
along with the song-notes of partridges,
and crows.
                    Sometimes organization
and computation become absurd.

(*Mathnawi*, II, 1680-1708)

Four Indians enter a mosque and begin the prostrations.
Deep, sincere praying. But a priest walks by,
and one of the Indians, without thinking, says,
"Oh, are you going to give the call to prayers now?
Is it time?"

The second Indian, under his breath,
"You spoke. Now your prayers are invalid."

The third, "Uncle, don't scold *him*!
You've done the same thing. Correct yourself."

The fourth, also out loud, "Praise to God,
I haven't made the mistake of these three."

So all four prayers are interrupted,
with the three fault-finders more at fault
than the original speaker!

Blessed is one who sees his weakness,
and blessed is one who, when he sees a flaw
in someone else, takes responsibility for it.

Because, half of any person is wrong and weak and off the path.
Half! The other half is dancing and swimming and flying
in the Invisible Joy.

You have ten open sores on your head. Put what salve
you have on yourself. Point out to everyone
the dis-ease you are. That's part of getting well!

When you lance yourself that way, you become
                more merciful,
and wiser. Even if you don't have some particular
                fault
at the moment, you may soon become the one
who makes that very act notorious.

Don't feel self-satisfied.
Satan lived eons as a noble angel.
Think what that name means now.
Don't try to be famous until your face
is completely washed of all fear.
If your beard hasn't grown out,
don't joke about someone's smooth chin.

Consider how Satan swallowed soul-poison,
and be grateful that you taste only
the sweetness of being warned.

(*Mathnawi*, II, 3027-3045)

Some gnats come from the grass to speak with Solomon.

"O Solomon, you are the champion of the oppressed.
You give justice to the little guys, and they don't get
any littler than us! We are tiny metaphors
for frailty. Can you defend us?"

"Who has mistreated you?"

"Our complaint is against the wind."

"Well," says Solomon, "you have pretty voices,
you gnats, but remember, a judge cannot listen
to just one side. I must hear both litigants."

"Of course," agree the gnats.

"Summon the East Wind!" calls out Solomon,
and the wind arrives almost immediately.

What happened to the gnat plaintiffs? Gone.

Such is the way of every seeker who comes to complain
at the High Court. When the Presence of God arrives,
where are the seekers? First there's dying,
then Union, like gnats inside the wind.

(*Mathnawi* , III, 4624-4633, 4644-4659)

B orrow the Beloved's eyes.
Look through them and you'll see the Beloved's face
everywhere. No tiredness, no jaded boredom.
"I shall be your eye and your hand and your loving."
Let that happen, and things
you have hated will become helpers.

A certain preacher always prays long and with enthusiasm
for thieves and muggers that attack people
on the street. "Let your mercy, O Lord,
cover their insolence."
He doesn't pray for the good,
but only for the blatantly cruel.
Why is this?   his congregation asks.

"Because they have done me such generous favors.
Every time I turn back toward the things they want.
I run into them. They beat me and leave me nearly dead
in the road, and I understand, again, that what they want
is not what I want. They keep me on the spiritual path.
That's why I honor them and pray for them."

Those that make you return, for whatever reason,
to God's solitude, be grateful to them.
Worry about the others, who give you
delicious comforts that keep you from prayer.
Friends are enemies sometimes,
and enemies Friends.

There is an animal called an *ushghur*, a porcupine.
If you hit it with a stick, it extends its quills
and gets bigger. The soul is a porcupine,
made strong by stick-beating.

52

So a prophet's soul is especially afflicted,
because it has to become so powerful.

A hide is soaked in tanning liquor and becomes leather.
If the tanner did not rub in the acid,
the hide would get foul-smelling and rotten.

The soul is a newly-skinned hide, bloody and gross.
Work on it with manual discipline,
and the bitter tanning-acid of grief,
and you'll become lovely, and *very* strong.

If you can't do this work yourself, don't worry.
You don't even have to make a decision,
one way or another. The Friend, who knows
a lot more than you do, will bring difficulties,
and grief, and sickness,
                           as medicine, as happiness,
as the essence of the moment when you're beaten,
when you hear *Checkmate*, and can finally say,
with Hallaj's voice,
                   I trust you to kill me.

(*Mathnawi*, IV, 74-109)

I f your name is Omar, nobody in the town of Kash
will sell you a loaf of bread, at *any* price.

You go to a bakery shop and say, "Hello, my name is Omar.
I'd like some bread." The baker will reply, "Try the shop
down the street. One loaf of his is better than fifty of mine."

But if you have healed your eyesight of all duality,
you can answer, "There is no other bakery!"
The illumination of that would blind the baker
and change your name.

As it is, the bakers of Kash nod, and with tones of voice
they know, send you on a wild-goose chase around town.

Once you have said your name is "Omar" in one shop,
you may as well quit trying to buy bread in Kash.
You're not only seeing double. You're seeing ten-fold!
And you'll never get fed.

You move from nook to nook in the ruins of a monastery,
thinking, *The next prayer-place is the place I'm looking for.*

Let your eyes see God everywhere. Give up fears
and expectations. The Friend, the Beloved, your Soul,
is a River with the trees and buds of the world
reflected in it. And it's no illusion!

The reflections are real, real images, through which
God is made real to you. This River Water
is an orchard that fills your basket. Be splashed!

But not all flowings are the same. Different donkeys
take different loads and different persuasive sticks.
One principle does not apply to all rivers.

For example, inside this River there is a Moon
which is not a reflection!

From the riverbottom the Moon speaks,
                              "I travel
in continuous conversation with the River as it goes.
Whatever is above and seemingly outside this River
is actually *in* it. It all belongs to the Friend."

Merge with it, in here or out there, as you please,
because this is the River of Rivers
and the Beautiful Silence of Endless Talking.

(*Mathnawi*, VI, 3220-3246)

Don't go to sleep one night.
What you most want will come to you then.
Warmed by a sun inside, you'll see wonders.

Tonight, don't put your head down.
Be tough, and strength will come.
That which adoration adores
appears at night. Those asleep
may miss it. One night Moses stayed awake
and asked, and saw a light in a tree.

Then he walked at night for ten years,
until finally he saw the whole tree
illuminated. Muhammed rode his horse
through the nightsky. The day is for work.
The night for love. Don't let someone
bewitch you. Some people sleep at night.

But not lovers. They sit in the dark
and talk to God, who told David,
Those who sleep all night every night
and claim to be connected to us, they lie.

Lovers can't sleep when they feel the privacy
of the Beloved all around them. Someone
who's thirsty may sleep for a little while,
but he or she will dream of water, a full jar
beside a creek, or the spiritual water you get
from another person. All night, listen
to the Conversation.

Stay up. This moment is all there is.
Death will take it away soon enough.
You'll be gone, and this earth will be left
without a sweetheart, nothing but weeds
growing inside thorns.

I'm through. Read the rest of this poem
in the dark tonight.
                    Do I have a head? And feet?

Shams, so loved by Tabrizians, I close my lips.
I wait for you to come and open them.

(#258)

P ain comes from seeing
how arrogant you've been, and pain
brings you out of that conceit.

A child cannot be born
until the mother has pain.

You are pregnant with real trusting.
The words of the prophets and saints are midwives
to help, but first you must feel pain.

To be without pain is to use the first person wrongly.
"I" am this, "I" am that.
"I" am God like al-Hallaj,
who waited till that was true to say it.

"I" at the wrong time brings a curse.
"I" at the right time gives a blessing.
If a rooster crows early, when it's still dark,
he must have his head cut off.

What is this beheading?
As one might extract a scorpion's sting
to save it, or a snake's venom
to keep it from being stoned, headlessness
comes from your cleansing connection
to a teacher. Hold to a true Sheikh.
Strength will come. Your strength
is his gathering you closer.

Soul of the Soul of the Soul, moment to moment,
hope to draw breath from that ONE.

No matter if you've been long apart.
That Presence has no absence in it.

Do you want to understand more about such Friendship?
Read many times the Sura called *Daybreak.*

(*Mathnawi* , II, 2817-2834)

Yesterday was glory and joy.
Today, a blackened burn everywhere.

On the record of my life, these two days
will be put down as *one.*

(#1881)

Last night, full of longing, asking
the wine-woman for more, and then more.

She teased me so lovingly I fell
into her and disappeared. Then
she was there alone.

(#1878)

Last night you left me and slept
your own deep sleep. Tonight you turn
and turn. I say,
"You and I will be together
till the Universe dissolves."

You mumble back things you thought of
when you were drunk.

(#1879)

So delicate yesterday, the nightsinging birds by the creek. Their words were:

You may make a jewelry flower
out of gold and rubies and emeralds,
but it will have no fragrance.

(#1880)

I come to you, aching for you.
You say, "You're drunk.
Go away."

I say, "No. I'm not drunk.
Please open the door." You say,
"You are, you *are*..
Go away."

(#1885)

I went to the Doctor. "I feel lost, blind with love. What should I do?"

Give up owning things and being somebody. Quit existing.

(#1886)

You are the pump of my pulse,
so the good or bad I do is due
to you.
    Now my eyesight's going,
which is also your fault, since
you're the lightpoints in my eyes!

(#1876)

Muhammed says,
"I come before dawn
to chain you and drag you off."
It's amazing, and funny, that you have to be pulled away
from being tortured, pulled out
into this Spring garden,
but that's the way it is.

Almost everyone must be bound and dragged here.
Only a few come on their own.

Children have to be made to go to school at first.
Then some of them begin to like it.
They run to school.
They expand with the learning.
Later, they receive money
because of something they've learned at school,
and they get really excited. They stay up all night,
as watchful and alive as thieves!

Remember the rewards you get for being obedient!

There are two types on the Path. Those who come
against their will, the blindly religious people, and those
who obey out of love. The former have ulterior motives.
They want the Midwife near, because she gives them milk.
The others love the Beauty of the Nurse.

The former memorize the proof-texts of conformity,
and repeat them. The latter disappear
into whatever draws them to God.

Both are drawn from the Source.
Any moving's from the Mover.
Any love from the Beloved.

(Mathnawi, III, 4587-4600)

A man on his deathbed left instructions
for dividing up his goods among his three sons.
He had devoted his entire spirit to those sons.
They stood like cypress trees around him,
quiet and strong.
                    He told the town judge,
"Whichever of my sons is *laziest,*
give him *all* the inheritance."

Then he died, and the judge turned to the three,
"Each of you must give some account of your laziness,
so I can understand just *how* you are lazy."

Gnostics are experts in laziness. They rely on it,
because they continuously see God working all around them.
The harvest keeps coming in, yet they
never even did the ploughing!

"Come on. Say something about the ways you are lazy."

Every spoken word is a covering for the inner self.
A little curtain-flick no wider than a slice
of roast meat can reveal hundreds of exploding suns.
Even if what is being said is trivial and wrong,
the listener hears the source. One breeze comes
from across a garden. Another from across the ash-heap.
Think how different the voices of the fox
and the lion, and what they tell you!

Hearing someone is lifting the lid off the cooking pot.
You learn what's for supper. Though some people
can know just by the smell, a sweet stew
from a sour soup cooked with vinegar.

A man taps a clay pot before he buys it
to know by the sound if it has a crack.

The eldest of the three brothers told the judge,
"I can know a man by his voice,
                                    and if he won't speak,
I wait three days, and then I know him intuitively."

The second brother, "I know him when he speaks,
and if he won't talk, I strike up a conversation."

"But what if he knows that trick?" asked the judge.

Which reminds me of the mother who tells her child,
"When you're walking through the graveyard at night
and you see a boogeyman, run *at* it,
and it will go away."

"But what," replies the child,"if the boogeyman's
mother has told it to do the same thing?
Boogeymen have mothers too."

The second brother had no answer.

The judge then asked the youngest brother,
"What if a man cannot be made to say anything?

How do you learn his hidden nature?"

"I sit in front of him in silence,
and set up a ladder made of patience,
and if in his presence a language from beyond joy
and beyond grief begins to pour from my chest,
I know that his soul is as deep and bright
as the star Canopus rising over Yemen.

And so when I start speaking a powerful right arm
of words sweeping down, I know *him* from what *I* say,
and how I say it, because there's a window open
between us, mixing the night air of our beings."

The youngest was, obviously,
the laziest. He won.

(*Mathnawi*, VI, 4876-4916)

This is the story of the lake and the three big fish
that were in it, one of them intelligent,
another half-intelligent,

                and the third, stupid.

Some fisherman came to the edge of the lake
with their nets. The three fish saw them.

The intelligent fish decided at once to leave,
to make the long, difficult trip to the ocean.

He thought,
           "I won't consult with these two on this.
They will only weaken my resolve, because they love
this place so. They call it *home*. Their ignorance
will keep them here."

When you're traveling, ask a traveler for advice,
not someone whose lameness keeps him in one place.

Muhammed says,
           "Love of one's country
is part of the Faith."
           But don't take that literally!
Your real "country" is where you're heading,
not where you *are*.
           Don't misread that *hadith* .

 In the ritual ablutions, according to Tradition,
there's a separate prayer for each body-part.
When you snuff water up your nose to cleanse it,
beg for the scent of the Spirit. The proper prayer is,
"Lord, wash me. My hand has washed this part of me,
but *my* hand can't wash my spirit.

72

I can wash this skin,
but You must wash ME."

A certain man used to say the wrong prayer
for the wrong hole. He'd say the nose-prayer
when he splashed his behind. Can the odor of heaven
come from our rumps? Don't be humble with fools.
Don't take pride into the Presence of a Spiritual Master.

It's right to love your Home Place, but first ask,
Where is that, really?

The wise fish saw the men and their nets and said,
"I'm leaving."

Ali was told a secret doctrine by Muhammed
and told not to tell it, so he whispered it down
the mouth of a well. Sometimes there's no one to talk to.
You must just set out on your own.

So the intelligent fish made its whole length
a moving footprint and, like a deer the dogs chase,
suffered greatly on its way, but finally made it
to the edgeless safety of the sea.

The half-intelligent fish thought,
                                    "My Guide
has gone. I ought to have gone with him,
but I didn't, and now I've lost my chance
to escape.
            I wish I'd gone with him."

Don't regret what's happened. If it's in the past,
let it go. Don't even *remember* it!

A certain man caught a bird in a trap.
The bird says, "Sir, you have eaten many cows and sheep
in your life, and you're still hungry. The little bit
of meat on my bones won't satisfy you either.
If you let me go, I'll give you three pieces of wisdom.
One I'll say standing on your hand. One on your roof.
And one I'll speak from the limb of that tree."

The man was interested. He freed the bird and let it stand
on his hand.
                "Number One: Do not believe an absurdity,
no matter who says it."

The bird flew and lit on the man's roof. "Number Two:
Do not grieve over what is past. It's over.
Never regret what has happened."

"By the way," the bird continued, "in my body there's a huge
pearl weighing as much as ten copper coins. It was meant
to be the inheritance of you and your children,
but now you've lost it. You could have owned
the largest pearl in existence, but evidently,
it was not meant to be."

The man started wailing like a woman in childbirth.
The bird, "Didn't I just say, *Don't grieve
for what's in the past?* And also, *Don't believe
an absurdity?* My entire body doesn't weigh
as much as ten copper coins. How could I have
a pearl that heavy inside me?"

The man came to his senses. "All right.
Tell me Number Three."

"Yes. You've made such good use of the first two!"

Don't give advice to someone who's groggy
and falling asleep. Don't throw seeds on the sand.
Some torn places cannot be patched.

Back to the second fish,
                    the half-intelligent one.
He mourns the absence of his Guide for a while,
and then thinks, "What can I do to save myself
from these men and their nets? Perhaps if I pretend
to be already dead!
                    I'll belly up on the surface
and float like weeds float, just giving myself totally
to the water. To die before I die, as Muhammed
said to."
            So he did that.

He bobbed up and down, helpless,
within arm's reach of the fishermen.

"Look at this! The best and biggest fish
is dead."
            One of the men lifted him by the tail,
spat on him, and threw him up on the ground.

He rolled over and over and slid secretly near
the water, and then, back in.

Meanwhile,
the third fish, the dumb one, was agitatedly
jumping about, trying to escape with his agility
and cleverness.
                    The net, of course, finally closed
around him, and as he lay in the terrible
frying-pan bed, he thought,
                                    "If I get out of this,
I'll never live again in the limits of a lake.
Next time, the Ocean! I'll make
the Infinite my Home."

(*Mathnawi*,   IV, 2203-2286)

A poet began to sing at a banquet.
He sang directly to God in the state of *Alast*,
the primal covenant between God and Man in Pre-Existence.

Under the cover of words and melody
he sang to the drunken Turks
from inside that Mystery.

> *I do not know what You are, or what*
> *You want of me. What service, what words.*
> *How You draw me to You. With the Moon?*
> *With blood? I do not know,*
> > *I do not know.*
>
> *I do not know.*

> *I do not know.*

All he could do was open his lips and let

> *I do not know*

come out.
> The chief drunk jumped up and grabbed
an iron mace.
> "This guy is getting on my nerves.
I'll knock him in the head and stop this repeating.

If you don't know, asshole, shut up this nonsense!
Say something you *do* know, like where are you from!

You'll say,
          Not from Balkh,
                    not from Herat,
                              not Baghdad,
not Mosul, not Tiraz,
                    Not, Not, taking us all over the world.

What did you have for breakfast?
                              Not roast beef, not
a glass of wine,
                    not strips of kabob, not
bread soaked in gravy,
                    not lentils.
                              Just tell me
one positive thing and quit!
                    Why all this not-not-ing?"

"Because until you deny *every* thing, God escapes you.
I play the tune of NO to get to YES. You suffer,
but not enough to die. Your ladder is missing
two rungs, so you can't reach the roof.
The well-rope is one yard short of the water.

Your ship will not sink,
until you put the last sixteen pound stone
in it.
          That last stone

is the piercing star that comes up at night
and makes you act.

When the ship of consciousness sinks,
it becomes the blue vault of the sky
with the sun inside it.

You have not died. Your suffering continues.
Be extinguished in the dawn,

lovely candle of Tiraz!

All our stars must hide as the Sun comes up.
Hit yourself with the mace. Shatter ego.
Your body-eye is a cotton wad in your ear.

If fact, you *are* attacking yourself.
You see yourself in the mirror of me,
like the lion who creeps down the well
to attack his likeness.

There is no way, at this time,
to make God known except by denying

the not-God."

Die to how you are.
Childhood dies and becomes maturity.
Some of the ground dies and turns to gold. Sadness
changes into joy.

Muhammed says, "If you want to see
a dead man walking around living, look at Abu Bakr.
Look at such a one,

and believe in Resurrection."

(*Mathnawi*, VI, 703-749)

A long cry at midnight near the mosque,
                    a dying cry.
The young man sitting there hears
and thinks, "That sound doesn't make me afraid.
Why should it?
                    It's the drumbeat announcing a celebration!
It means,
              we should start cooking the joy-soup!"

He hears beyond his death-fear, to the Union.
"It's time for that Merging in me now,
or it's time to leave my body."

He jumps up and shouts to God,
If You can be human, come inside me now!

The signal of a death-yell splits him open.
Gold pours down, many kinds, from all directions,
gold coins, liquid gold, gold cloth, gold bars.
They pile up, almost blocking the doors of the mosque.

The young man works all night carrying the gold away
in sacks and burying it, and coming back for more.
The timid church-members sleep through it all.

If you think I'm talking about actual gold,
you're like those children who pretend that pieces
of broken dishes are money, so that anytime they see
pottery shards, they think of money, as when you hear
the word *gold* and think "Goody."

This is the other gold
that glows in your chest when you love.

The enchanted mosque is in *there* , and the pointed cry
is a candleflame on the altar.
                       The young man is a moth
who gambles himself and wins. A True Human Being
is not human! This candle does not burn.
                                      It illuminates.

Some candles burn themselves, and one another, up.
Others taste like a surprise of roses in a room,
and you just a stranger who wandered in.

(*Mathnawi* , III, 4345-4374)

Listen to the poet Sanai,
who lived secluded, "Don't wander out on the road
in your ecstasy. Sleep in the tavern."

When a drunk strays out to the street,
children make fun of him.
                              He falls down in the mud.
He takes any and every road.
                              The children follow,
not knowing the taste of wine, or how
his drunkenness feels. All people on the planet
are children,
                    except for a very few.
No one is grown up except those free of desire.

God said,
              "The world is a play, a children's game,
and you are the children."
                              God speaks the Truth.
If you haven't left the child's play,
how can you be an adult?
                              Without purity of spirit,
if you're still in the middle of lust and greed
and other wantings, you're like children
playing at sexual intercourse.
                              They wrestle
and rub together, but it's not sex!

The same with the fightings of mankind.
It's a children's quarrel with play-swords.
No purpose, totally futile.

Like kids on hobby horses, soldiers claim to be riding
Boraq, Muhammed's night-horse, or Duldul, his mule.

Your actions mean nothing, the sex and war that you do.
You're holding part of your pants and prancing around,
Dun-da-dun, dun-da-dun.

Don't wait till you die to see this.
Recognize that your imagination and your thinking
and your sense-perception are reed canes
that children cut and pretend are horsies.

The Knowing of mystic Lovers is different.
The empirical, sensory, sciences
are like a donkey loaded with books,
or like the makeup woman's makeup.

                                        It washes off.
But if you lift the baggage rightly, it will give joy.
Don't carry your knowledge-load for some selfish reason.
Deny your desires and willfulness,
and a real mount may appear under you.

Don't be satisfied with the *name* of HU,
with just words about it.

Experience *That Drunkenness.*
From books and words come fantasy,
and sometimes, from fantasy
comes UNION.

(*Mathnawi,* I, 3426-3454)

A certain person came to the Friend's door
and knocked.
                    "Who's there?
"It's me."

The Friend answered, "Go away. There's no place
for raw meat at this table."

The individual went wandering for a year.
Nothing but the fire of separation
can change hypocrisy and ego. The person returned
completely cooked,
walked up and down in front of the Friend's house,
gently knocked.
                    "Who is it?"

"You."

"Please come in, my Self,
there's no place in this house for two.
The doubled end of the thread is not what goes through
the eye of the needle.
It's a single-pointed, fined-down, thread-end,
not a big ego-beast with baggage."

But how can a camel be thinned to a thread?
With the shears of practices, with *doing* things.

And with help from the ONE who brings
impossibilities to pass, who quiets willfulness,
who gives sight to one blind from birth.

Every Day That ONE Does Something.
Take that as your text.

Every day God sends forth three powerful energies:
One, from the sperm of the father into the mother,
so growth may begin.
Two, a birth from the womb of the ground,
so male and female may spring into existence.
Three, there's a surge up from the surface
into what is beyond dying, that the real beauty
of Creating can be recognized.

There's no way to ever say this.

Let's return to the two Friends whose thread
became single,
                   who spell with their two letters
the original word,
                   BE.

B and E tighten around subjects and objects
that one knot may hold them. Two scissor-blades
make one cut.
                   And watch two men washing clothes.
One makes dry clothes wet. The other makes
wet clothes dry. They seem to be thwarting each other,
but their work is a perfect harmony.

Every holy person seems to have a different doctrine
and practice, but there's really only one work.

Someone listening to a millstone falls asleep.
No matter. The stone keeps turning.

Water from the mountain
far above the mill keeps flowing down.
The sleepers will get their bread.

Underground it moves, without sound, and without
repetition. Show us where that source of speech is
that has no alphabet. That spaciousness.

Where we are now is a narrow fantasy
that comes from there, and the actual, outside world
is even narrower. Narrowness is pain,
and the cause of narrowness is many-ness.

Creation was spoken with one sound, *BE.*
The two letters, B and E,
                              to record it,
came after.
                    The meaning of the Sound
and its Resonance
                         are ONE.

There's no way to ever say this,
in *so many words!*   And no place
to stop saying it.

Meanwhile, a lion and a wolf were fighting....

(*Mathnawi* , I, 3065-3101)

Acknowledgements

I have had good help putting this book together, both in its original form, and in this longer form.

Many thanks to, and blessings on, Phyllis Cole of Menlo Park, and Andrew Dick of Madison, Wisconsin, and Michael and Sally Green of Philadelphia, and David Huebner of Chicago, who did the cover painting.